Woh Dhai Din

THOSE 2½ DAYS IN
BENARAS

MAHESH GOKLANI

ISBN

Paperback 979-8-89724-521-5

Hardcase 979-8-89906-580-4

CONTENTS

PRAISE FOR THE BOOK

Hey Mahesh!

So happy to read that your book is ready to print

I must say, it's such a heartfelt and beautiful story.

The way you brought Benaras to life was amazing! I could almost feel the ghats, the aarti, and the spiritual vibe. Your descriptions made me want to visit the place.

The story of Simran and Rahul is so relatable and emotional. The way you've captured their reunion after 40 years felt very real and touching.

One thing I really appreciated is how you've shown the importance of living in the moment and cherishing connections. It's something we all need to remember.

I loved how the story unfolds. It's a reminder of how destiny works in unexpected ways. You've done a great job, and it's clear how much heart you've poured into it.

Proud of you, buddy! Looking forward to more stories from you. Keep writing!

– Niyati Shah

Intimacy Coach, Author

Mahesh has penned a beautiful synthesis of a romantic travelogue where the protagonist and places have been brought to life succinctly and lucidly.

– Vikram Nankani

Senior Advocate

Woh Dhai Din Aur Zindagi Bhar Ki Yaadein

The book will not disappoint you if you are a lover of romance, history, culture and India. The story navigates beautifully through the gullies of Benares, weaving its magic from the temples of Kashi Vishwanath with its ode to Lord Shiva to the Ghats with its mesmerizing spirituality that acts as a soothing balm to deeply disturbed souls.

Maheshji shows not only his prowess with words in this beautiful saga, but proves himself to be a master of a destination that he so clearly loves – Benares. The description of each place is so vivid that you will feel as though you are right there, viewing at what the protagonists are viewing in the novel, feeling what they are feeling and being who they are being at that moment.

The sweet romance between Rahul and Simran that spans over several decades is a reminder of all that was simple and pure in yonder days, where a glance was more passionate than a caress and a smile evoked more desire than a kiss. The book is pure nostalgia with wisps of hope, dream and faith deeply intertwined and enmeshed together.

Maheshji once again delights us with one more colour to his already satrangi personality. As you will read the book, you will love how the phrases flow like water over rocks and cascade with music that resonates in your ears till long after.

Maheshji has woven together all that is part of his personality – music, romance, creativity, love for travel and way with words in this wonderful book.

Each detail will evoke in you a desire to make Benares the next destination in your Bucket List, as it has done with mine.

My deepest gratitude to Maheshji for making me a part of his journey and my best wishes for the new one that he has started.

– Vijayalakshmi Suvarna

MD and CEO – Liberation Coaches Pvt. Ltd.

Independent Director – Gopal Snacks Ltd.

Independent Director – LCC Projects Ltd.

Author, International Speaker, Empowerment Coach

Dear Mahesh,

I just finished reading Woh Dhai Din, and I loved it. The characters feel real, and their relationships — both subtle and direct — are beautifully portrayed.

Thank you for sharing your manuscript. The story keeps you hooked, blending a tender tale of love with the charm and history of Benaras.

In just two and a half days, something unexpected unfolds — a moment of true transformation, showing the power of friendship.

This story will touch hearts across all ages — it's bittersweet, emotional, and may even bring a tear, but it will definitely leave you smiling. It's a Must Read.

Wishing you all the best in this new journey. You are truly multi-talented, and it's wonderful to see you putting your gifts to such good use. May this be the first of many successful books to come.

With love and blessings to you, Rati, and your lovely family,

– Godafrid Mistry
Retired Banker

Kashi, or Varanasi, is a city I have long had mixed emotions about. My first visit at 14 left me overwhelmed by the chaos — the dirty river, the narrow lanes — and yet, something about it fascinated me. When I returned two decades later, the city hadn't changed much, but I saw it with new eyes. What captivated me then was its sheer antiquity — a city shaped by centuries of saints and sinners, kings and commoners, each leaving their mark.

Reading Mahesh's book brought back all those memories. His story isn't just about the city's famous temples and ghats, but about the people who bring it to life — including his two main characters. Through them, the city becomes more than a backdrop; it is a living, breathing presence. For those who know Kashi, the book stirs nostalgia. For those who don't, it inspires curiosity.

"For me, it revived my yearning to go back — to lose myself once more in those ancient lanes and the stories they still keep."

– Anuradha Shankar,

Blogger and Freelance Travel Writer

Woh Dhai Din is a beautiful blend of relationships and learnings of life set in backgrounds of history and divinity.

Written so simply yet underscores the importance of being happy in every situation by learning to accept and overcome challenges of life.

– Prasad Dhande

Advocate High Court

Acknowledgements

At the very outset, I offer my deepest gratitude and reverence to my Divine Master, Bhagawan Shiva, for blessing me with the opportunity to visit His sacred abode, Kashi.

My heartfelt appreciation goes to my dearest wife, Rati, for her unwavering support, patience, and encouragement throughout my journey of writing this book. A special thanks to my sons, Sai Satish Goklani and Sai Paresh Goklani, for their invaluable feedback, meticulous review of drafts, and creative contributions to the book's design.

I am profoundly grateful to my friend and fellow author, Niyati Shah, for her invaluable guidance, insightful feedback during the process and thoughtful review. A special note of appreciation to my dear friend and guide, Vijaya Suvana, whose wisdom, unwavering support, and contributions to the reviews have been truly inspiring.

I extend my sincere thanks to Vikram Nankani, a cherished friend and well-wisher, as well as Anuradha Shankar, my blogging mentor, for their encouragement. My gratitude also goes to my musical friends, Godafrid Mistry (Guddi) and Prasad

Dhande, for their thoughtful reviews and constant encouragement.

I also wish to acknowledge my dear friends—Sukhbir, Ravi, Shailesh, Omesh, and Anil—whose efforts were instrumental in planning and ensuring the success of this spiritual visit.

A special word of thanks to Mr. Arun, who graciously guided us through the intricate bylanes of the holy city, enriching our experience with his knowledge and warmth.

Last but certainly not least, my sincere gratitude to my publishing team from Notion Press, Ranjali, Riyaa, Manisha, Lajja, and Sooraj—for their dedication, hard work, and sincere efforts in bringing this book to life.

This book is a culmination of the love, support, and encouragement of all these incredible individuals. To each of you, I am deeply grateful.

PREFACE

I've always believed in the power of stories to connect us with emotions, places, and people we might never encounter otherwise. "Woh Dhai Din" is my attempt to capture not just a fleeting moment of love, but the deep and timeless connections that can form when fate has its say.

Benaras, with its rich history, spiritual depth, and unhurried pace, is the heart of this story. It is a city that speaks in whispers, where every lane and every Ghat carries a memory. In this city, two people, who were once schoolmates and strangers to each other's dreams, rediscover themselves and each other after four decades. I often think about how life has a way of leading us to places we never expect, even after years of separation.

"Woh Dhai Din" is not just about romance—it's about rediscovering one's roots, reconnecting with the past, and realising that some moments, even if brief, can change the course of our lives forever. Rahul and Simran's journey is one of self-reflection and hope. It reminds us that it's never too late to experience the joy of new beginnings, even if those beginnings are deeply intertwined with old memories.

This book is a tribute to the beauty of serendipity, the wisdom of life's experiences, and the grace of human connections. I hope it touches your heart, as it has mine, and leaves you with a sense of wonder about how life, even in its later years, continues to surprise us with the possibility of love, growth, and redemption.

Thank you for reading, and I hope you find in "Woh Dhai Din" a story that resonates with your own experiences of connection, reflection, and, most importantly, the joy of rediscovering what truly matters.

– Mahesh Goklani

PRELUDE

DESTINY

The plan had been meticulously organised months in advance, Benaras, Prayagraj, Ayodhya, and Lucknow, all from the sacred aarti to the sightseeing, from savouring the city's legendary street food to immersing in its rich culture. But what unfolded during those two and a half days in Benaras was far beyond any human planning. *A tale destined by the divine, a script written by fate for **Simran** and **Rahul**.*

Simran and Rahul, now in their mid-fifties, were distant strangers tied by the faint memories of a shared past.

Forty years had passed since their schooldays, a time marked by youthful innocence. Back then, their bond was simple — exchanging books, passing notes, and sharing fleeting glances that hinted at unspoken feelings neither had the courage to express. Rahul was the sincere boy next door — studious, grounded, and shyly approachable. Simran exuded quiet confidence, with a clear mind. Though they shared a silent camaraderie, their worlds within the same school remained apart, divided by their ambitions and the hesitance of youth.

As the final school bell rang and they stepped into adulthood, life pulled them onto separate paths. Rahul pursued commerce, building a stable career and a loving family with his wife and two children. Simran ventured into the world of science, her journey taking her into a life enriched by experiences and the family she built along the way. Though their lives were full in their own right, the faint memory of those school days lingered, buried beneath layers of time. Neither Rahul nor Simran had confessed the quiet affection they carried in their hearts during their youth. For them, it had been a time of restraint, where feelings were left unspoken, and dreams were shelved in favour of responsibilities. Yet, in the deepest corners of their memories, the other's presence remained, like a bookmark in a cherished novel they had long stopped reading.

And then, as if guided by the unseen hand of destiny, their stories converged again—this time in the sacred city of Benaras. A city, steeped in history, spirituality, and the mystique of timelessness, Benaras provided the perfect backdrop for a reunion that neither had anticipated.

It was here, amidst the ghats, the shimmering Ganges, and the chanting of prayers, that their paths crossed once more.

Rahul had come to Benaras for a break and to reconnect with himself. Simran was settled in Benaras. Their meeting was not orchestrated by plans or forethought; it was a serendipitous moment, a fleeting instance when the threads of their past intertwined with their present.

Standing on the steps of a Ghat, bathed in the golden hues of the setting sun, their eyes met. At first, there was disbelief, a hesitation to accept the impossible reality of the moment. But as recognition dawned, so did the flood of emotions—reminiscence, curiosity, and the warmth of a bond that had quietly endured the test of time. Their reunion was not just a meeting of old friends; it was a testament to the unpredictability of life and the power of connections that refuse to fade. In Benaras, where every moment seems to echo with eternity, they were given a rare gift: the chance to revisit their shared past, rediscover themselves, and perhaps, redefine what they meant to each other in the present.

Destiny had brought them back together, and the sacred city, with its timeless grace, had become the keeper of their second chapter.

THE REUNION

It was during the aarti at Assi Ghat on the evening of 3rd December 2024 that their paths converged. The chants of the priests, the rhythmic beating of drums, and the golden glow of the lamps mirrored the turbulence and anticipation that suddenly gripped Rahul's heart. Amid the crowd, he saw a familiar face.

At first, he hesitated. Could it really be her? Gathering courage, he approached the woman.

"Simran?" he asked hesitantly.

She turned, her eyes widening in recognition. *"Rahul?"* She replied, almost as if time itself had paused for them.

Soon they were seated across each other at Kashi Café. **Rahul's** curiosity was palpable as he leaned forward. *"Do you remember me?"*

Simran smiled warmly. *"Of course, I do. How could I forget?"*

Rahul was overwhelmed, his emotions surging like a tidal wave. The sight of Simran, sitting before him after all these years, stirred a whirlwind of curiosity and longing. Memories of their school days blended with the undeniable need to know her story—what life had been like for her during the decades they had been apart. It was as if the clock had rewound, placing him in the role of an eager schoolboy, yearning to learn everything about his old friend.

He couldn't hold back the cascade of questions:

"Where have you been all these years?

What have you done?

Are you happy?

How has life treated you?"

His voice was a mix of excitement, concern, and a deep-seated desire to bridge the vast gap that time had carved between them.

Simran, however, remained composed, her serene smile reflecting her wisdom and maturity. She answered a few of his initial questions, her words measured and warm.

She spoke briefly about her life, her family, and the path she had walked, offering him glimpses into her world. But she soon noticed Rahul's intensity, the urgency in his voice, and the rapidity of his questions.

Gently, she placed a hand on his arm, a gesture both calming and reassuring. Her eyes met his, their gaze steady and understanding. *"Rahul,"* she said, her voice soft yet firm,

"We have time. Let's not rush." Her words carried a profound truth that stilled the moment. She let out a soft laugh, one that held the weight of years gone by but also the lightness of rediscovery. *"We have 40 years to catch up on,"* she continued, her tone playful yet comforting, *"and I promise, we will."*

Rahul leaned back, her words settling over him like a warm embrace. For the first time since their meeting, he allowed himself to pause, to take in the simplicity of their reunion without the pressure of the unspoken years. He smiled back, a hint of embarrassment in his expression, and nodded. "You're right," he admitted, his voice quieter now. *"I just... I can't believe you're here. After all this time."*

Simran's smile deepened, her eyes reflecting a mix of affection and patience. *"I'm here, Rahul,"* she said softly. *"And so are you. That's what matters. Let's take it one moment at a time."*

With that, the rush of the past gave way to the rhythm of the present. The urgency dissolved, leaving space for a more profound connection to grow. Their conversation slowed, unfolding naturally, like the gentle flow of the Ganges beside them. Time seemed to stretch and bend, allowing them to savour the richness of the moment, the beginning of a journey neither had anticipated but both were ready to embrace.

Rahul mentioned that we have just over 2 days with a soft smile. It seemed Simran missed this statement. Before parting that evening, they exchanged numbers. Simran left with a smile, leaving Rahul in a daze. He stood there, staring after her, feeling an inexplicable pull towards the past and the present all at once.

FRIENDLY FIRE

As Rahul returned to his hotel, he shared the highlights of his unexpected reunion with Simran at Assi Ghat.

"Guys," he began, a hint of excitement in his voice, *"while you all were busy exploring the streets of Benaras and chasing street food, I sneaked away to witness the Aarti. On my way, I bumped into someone — a school friend, Simran. At first, I wasn't sure it was her. But after mustering some courage, I approached her, and guess what? It was her! We talked and exchanged numbers, and I'm meeting her tomorrow."* His friends exchanged knowing glances before breaking into teasing laughter.

"Rahul, ditching the plan already for a school crush?!"

"Or should we say, rekindling old flames?" one of them quipped. *"Be careful, man,"* another chimed in, smirking. *You might not return to Mumbai with us!"*

Rahul sniggered, shaking his head. *"Alright, alright. Say what you want, but this is a once-in-a-lifetime coincidence. You guys continue with your plans — I'll catch up whenever possible."* The teasing continued, but Rahul just smiled, letting their jokes bounce off him.

That night, sleep eluded him. Questions buzzed in his mind, memories of their school days resurfacing like echoes from a distant era. His phone buzzed: a message from Simran. She had sent him the time and place for their next meeting.

DAY 1 : DISCOVERING BENARAS

Dawn in the Holy City

The boys were up early, eager to indulge in some of Benaras's famous delicacies. They headed straight to **Pehelwan Lassiwala**, Anand Baug, Lanka Road, renowned for its creamy lassi served in earthen pots. Along with the lassi, they savoured freshly made jalebi dripping with syrup and a generous serving of Rabri.

Pehelwan Lassiwala

Nearby, another gem awaited them—*Chachi Ki Kachori*, a local favourite. The crispy kachoris, paired with spicy potato curry, were a hit among the group. They devoured their plates, discussing the unique flavours and the charm of Benaras's food culture. Rahul, however, was more restrained. He took a small sip of the lassi and nibbled on a piece of jalebi.

"Not hungry, Rahul?" one of his friends asked, raising an eyebrow.

Rahul grinned. "Oh, I'm saving room. I have breakfast plans." Another round of playful jibes ensued, but Rahul didn't mind. He was looking forward to his meeting with Simran, curious about how the morning would unfold...

THE JOURNEY BEGINS – THE FIRST STEP FORWARD

Rahul was at the meeting spot sharp at 10:00 a.m. He saw her approaching, her figure framed against the morning sun, clad in an elegant Indian attire. Her smile was as radiant as the day before, and it felt as though the years between them dissolved in an instant.

Simran greeted him warmly.

"Good morning, Rahul. You're early." — *"I didn't want to waste a single minute."* said Rahul.

It was his first visit to Benaras, and he had a long list of places he had hoped to see. But now, none of it mattered. He told Simran about his plans, about his travel companions, four friends who were equally intrigued by their unexpected reunion. As this meeting marked their reunion after four decades, Simran was curious to understand Rahul's perspective on religious and spiritual matters. Gently, she asked, *'What are your thoughts on visiting the temples here in Benaras? There are thousands of them.'*

Rahul, with his characteristic ease, replied, *"I have no issues with visiting temples, but honestly, I'd much rather spend this time with you."*

Simran laughed and said with a playful smile, her voice ringing like a melodious tune. *"Don't worry; I'll take you to two temples that are a must-visit in Benaras. After that, we'll have plenty of time together."* Simran warmly said, *"First, we'll visit the Kaal Bhairav Temple, and then we'll head to the Kashi Vishwanath Temple."*

KAAL BHAIRAV TEMPLE

"Let me tell you about the Kaal Bhairav Temple," Simran stated, *"It's one of the most revered shrines in Benaras. Kaal Bhairav is considered the 'Kotwal,' or the guardian deity of the city. It's said that without his permission, no one can enter or leave this holy place."*

Her enthusiasm was contagious, drawing Rahul into the mystical stories of the ancient city they were about to explore together. Simran continued, her voice filled with reverence, *'The Kaal Bhairav Temple is truly special. It is a fierce form of Lord Shiva, and he is often referred to as the 'King of Kashi.' Legend says he was created by Shiva to destroy arrogance and evil.'*

People believe that he not only protects the city but also watches over its residents and visitors. Devotees come here to seek his blessings for courage, protection, and guidance.

Simran continued, "There is a fascinating tradition—*many believe that wearing a black thread blessed here wards off negativity and brings good fortune. The temple isn't just a place of worship; it's deeply woven into the lives of the people in Kashi. It's said that every visitor to the city must pay their respects to Kaal Bhairav to truly experience the blessings of Benaras."*

She paused, her eyes lighting up as she added, *"When we go there, you'll feel the energy – the mix of devotion, history, and spirituality."* It's like no other place.

With that, they set off – not just to explore the city, but to journey through the years they had lost, rediscovering each other one conversation at a time. And thus began the most unforgettable moments of their lives, as two old friends, separated by time but united by fate, rediscovered each other in the timeless city of Benaras.

As they walked through the labyrinthine lanes of Benaras, the city seemed to come alive with colours, aromas, and sounds. Rahul was struck by how effortlessly Simran navigated the chaos of the narrow streets, as though she belonged there.

Reaching the vicinity of the Kaal Bhairav Temple, a distinct energy enveloped them. The air was heavy with the aroma of incense and the sound of ringing bells. Devotees, some lost in deep prayer and others chanting hymns, created an atmosphere that felt both reverent and alive. The temple itself exuded an ancient charm, with its weathered walls speaking of countless years of devotion. The idol of Kaal Bhairav, fierce yet captivating, sat adorned with garlands of marigolds and offerings of mustard oil and black sesame seeds. His trident gleamed faintly in the flickering light of oil lamps. Simran whispered to Rahul, *"Do you feel it? That sense of awe – it's as if time stands still here."*

Rahul nodded, absorbing the profound serenity mingled with the temple's intensity. As they moved closer to offer their prayers, the priest tied a black thread around their wrists, chanting mantras for protection and strength.

Simran explained softly, *"This thread is a token of his guardianship, it's a connection to the divine, a shield of his presence with us."*

Stepping out of the temple into the bustling streets of Benaras, the experience lingered. Rahul, touched by the palpable spirituality of the place, remarked, *"There's an energy here that words can't capture. It's as if the temple breathes life into the city."*

Simran smiled and said, *now you see why I insisted we come here first.*

Rahul simply replied, *"I understand now. This is more than just a place – it's an experience."*

Simran nodded, her eyes reflecting a quiet joy. *"This is Kaal Bhairav's city, after all, to truly experience Kashi, one must begin here – with his blessings."* Together, they walked on, feeling as though the temple had opened a door not only to the city but also to a deeper understanding of their inner journey.

Simran smiled and said, *"Now, we proceed to the Kashi Vishwanath Temple. I hope you're not tired?"*

Rahul shook his head with a gentle grin and replied, *"Not at all, please lead the way."*.

Strolling through the vibrant streets of Benaras, the anticipation of visiting the sacred temple filled the air between them, blending seamlessly with the city's lively chaos.

Kashi Vishwanath Temple

Simran began, "Let me share with you the significance of the Kashi Vishwanath Temple, its history, and the recent developments. I'm sure you're not fully aware of its spiritual importance."

The Kashi Vishwanath Temple is one of India's most revered Hindu shrines, dedicated to Bhagawan Shiva, worshipped here as Vishwanath, the "Ruler of the Universe." It stands on the western bank of the sacred River Ganga and is of immense religious importance for Hindus. Benaras, or Varanasi, is regarded as one of the world's oldest living cities, and the Kashi Vishwanath Temple is its spiritual heart. Many pilgrims believe that a visit to this temple and offering prayers here can lead to salvation (moksha). The temple is one of the twelve Jyotirlingas of Shiva, considered sacred sites that symbolise Shiva's infinite presence.

Rahul listened attentively as he was unfamiliar with much of this information.

Simran went on, *"The temple boasts a magnificent gold-plated spire and dome, a gift from Maharaja Ranjit Singh in 1835. Over the centuries, it has been destroyed and rebuilt numerous times due to invasions. The current structure was constructed in 1780 by Rani Ahilyabai Holkar of Indore."*

"Adjacent to the temple stands the Gyanvapi Mosque, built by Mughal Emperor Aurangzeb. The Gyanvapi well within the mosque complex is considered sacred by devotees."

Rahul stated that he had read about Gyan Vapi.

Rahul mentioned *"It stands adjacent to the Kashi Vishwanath Temple. The mosque was constructed during the reign of the Mughal emperor Aurangzeb, by demolishing the original Vishweshwar Temple, which occupied the site. This act has made it a point of historical debate and cultural tension over the years. The name Gyanvapi translates to the "Well of Knowledge," referring to the sacred well located within the mosque complex, which is believed to be connected to the original temple."*

Simran acknowledged Rahul's reply and said, "Well, you are updated!"

Simran continued,

"The temple attracts thousands of visitors daily, especially during festivals such as Mahashivratri and Shravan. Devotional rituals like Rudra Abhishekam, where water, milk, and other offerings are made to the Shiva Linga, are performed with great reverence." And then Simran concluded, "Recently, the temple underwent a significant transformation with the Kashi Vishwanath Corridor project, which now connects the temple directly to the Ganges. I hope this gives you a comprehensive understanding of the temple's importance."

Soon, they reached Gate No. 4 of the Kashi Vishwanath Temple, the entry reserved for VIPs.

Simran smiled knowingly and handed over a pass to the temple officials. Rahul raised an eyebrow, his curiosity piqued.

"How did you manage this?" he asked, genuinely surprised.

Kashi Vishwanath Temple

Simran waved him off with a playful laugh. *"It's not important right now. Let's seek the Lord's blessings first. We can talk afterwards."* Rahul could not help but marvel at how different she seemed from the reserved girl he remembered from school. There was a confidence about her now, an aura of accomplishment. As they entered the temple, the serene chants and the fragrance of incense enveloped them, and Rahul found himself silently grateful for this moment.

Being a weekday, the temple wasn't crowded, and they completed the darshan within 15 minutes. The sight of the Shivling bathed in milk and flowers, and the rhythmic ringing of bells created a sense of peace that Rahul had not felt in years.

THE GRACIOUS HOST – MOMENTS SHARED, STORIES TOLD

As they stepped out of the temple, the soft chime of temple bells filled the air, mingling with the murmur of devotees. Simran turned to him, her eyes alight with a gentle smile.

"Are you satisfied with the Lord's darshan?" she asked, her voice calm yet filled with reverence.

He nodded, a serene expression softening his face. *"Completely. It felt... uplifting."*

Simran gestured towards a smaller shrine to their right. *"Let us pay our respects to Maa Annapoorna,"* she said, her tone both inviting and resolute. *"It is only fitting to seek her blessings for abundance and nourishment."*

Together, they began walking towards the shrine, their steps unhurried, as if savouring the sacredness of the moment.

Post darshan of the mother, Simran asked *"Have you had breakfast? You must be hungry by now."*

Rahul beamed. *"I guess you're the host now."*

She led him to a cosy South Indian restaurant within the temple complex. Over steaming plates of idli and dosa, their long-awaited conversation began.

"Tell me everything," Rahul said, leaning forward, his eyes eager. *"Start from where we left off."*

Simran paused for a moment, gathering her thoughts. *"After school, I joined the science stream, as you know. It was intense, 10 to 12 hours a day in college. I barely had time to breathe, let alone think about anything else."*

Rahul nodded, fully absorbed in every word.

"I worked hard and managed to secure a seat in Engineering at IIT Powai," she continued. *"It was during my time there that I met Raj. He was in my class, and we became close friends. He was a kind, intelligent boy, but his family struggled financially. That never mattered to me, though."* Rahul listened intently, noticing a flicker of emotion in her eyes.

"Raj and I supported each other through our studies," Simran said, her voice softening. *"By the time we*

graduated, we were inseparable. I got an opportunity to go to the United States for further studies, and Raj followed me there. Somewhere along the way, we realised we didn't want to live without each other."

Rahul raised an eyebrow. *"You got married in the US?"*

Simran nodded. *"Yes, actually, without my parents' approval. They were upset, furious. Raj's background was a problem for them, but I didn't bother. For me, he was enough. We built our lives together, step by step."*

There was a brief silence as Simran took a sip of her filter coffee. Rahul sensed that her story wasn't as simple as it seemed.

"Did things get better with your family?" He asked cautiously.

Simran sighed. *"Not immediately. It took quite a while for them to accept our marriage. By then, Raj and I were settled, and I was working in the tech industry, climbing the corporate ladder. Life was good, but..."*

Rahul waited, sensing the weight of unspoken words.

"But fate had its own plans," she said, her voice tinged with melancholy. *"Raj passed away," "A sudden illness. I was devastated, but I had to stay strong for my kids."*

Rahul reached out instinctively, placing a reassuring hand on hers. *"I'm so sorry, Simran. I can't even imagine what you've been through."*

She smiled faintly, her resilience shining through, the weight of her journey reflected in her eyes.

"Thank you, Rahul," she said softly. *"Life teaches us to endure, doesn't it? After Raj passed away, I poured all my energy into my work and raising my children. They've grown into fine individuals. My children have made me proud, my son is an IAS officer now, posted here in Benaras and my daughter is a medical doctor, happily married in Mumbai. And as for me, I've come full circle."*

Rahul tilted his head in curiosity. *"Full circle?"*

"Yes," she said, her voice steady yet tinged with emotion. *"I'm settled here in Benaras now, teaching technology at Benaras Hindu University (BHU). It's a quieter life, but it's fulfilling. This city... it has a way of healing you, doesn't it? There's something about its timelessness, its spiritual rhythm that soothes the soul."*

Rahul leaned back, marvelling at the transformation of the woman sitting across from him. The soft-spoken schoolgirl he had known had blossomed into a confident, accomplished woman. Her journey had been extraordinary, filled with love, loss, perseverance, and purpose.

"You've built a remarkable life, Simran," he said with genuine admiration. *"Teaching at BHU, raising an IAS officer and a doctor, finding peace in this ancient city, it's inspiring."*

Simran smiled, a glimmer of contentment in her expression. *"Thank you, Rahul. But life is less about what we achieve and more about how we grow through the challenges. I've learned to find beauty in the little things, to cherish the present."*

Rahul nodded, her words resonating deeply in his mind, *"And what about you? Have you found happiness again? Tell me."*

She paused, the question hanging in the air. Then, with a serene smile, she said, *"Happiness, Rahul, isn't always about finding something new. Sometimes, it's about embracing what you have, about making peace with your journey. Benaras has taught me that."*

For a moment, neither spoke. The bustling sounds of the temple complex faded into the background as they sat together, two old friends reconnecting not just with each other, but with the deeper truths of life.

Rahul felt a surge of admiration for Simran. The girl he had known as a quiet schoolmate had transformed into a woman of strength and grace, shaped by experiences he could barely fathom.

"You've come a long way, Simran," Rahul said softly.

"Enough about me," said Simran. *"It's your turn now, Rahul. Tell me about your life."*

And so, they began weaving together the threads of their stories, filling in the gaps of 40 years, one memory at a time. Benaras became more than a backdrop; it became a witness to their reconnection, a sacred space where the past and present converged.

THE HIDDEN SENTIMENTS

Rahul wanted to know more about Simran. His mind was teeming with questions, each one urging him to delve deeper into her story. He felt she had only scratched the surface, leaving the deeper truths hidden beneath. Gently, he prodded her to share everything in detail.

At first, Simran hesitated. Her expression wavered as if weighing whether to unburden herself or keep her past tucked away. But as the moments passed, and perhaps comforted by the serene ambiance of the Temple Corridor, she began. The quiet surroundings, free from interruptions, made it the perfect place for an unhurried conversation. With her hands wrapped around the warm cup of coffee, she started.

Simran began *"After my master's degree, my parents were adamant about me returning to India and getting me married,"* her voice steady but tinged with the faint echo of those pressures. *"There was a lot of pressure back then. They were traditional in their thinking, and they wanted to see me settled in a way they approved of."*

She paused, taking a sip of coffee before continuing. *"But I had someone in mind already — Raj. He was everything I wanted in a partner: kind, ambitious, and someone I truly understood. Convincing my parents wasn't easy. They wanted someone stable and settled. But Raj, after completing his post-graduation, landed a good job, and slowly, their resistance softened. They eventually accepted him as their son-in-law."*

Simran's face lit up momentarily as she recounted those early days. *"Raj and I both got great jobs in the US. Life felt perfect. We were building our dreams together. We were blessed with two children."*

Her voice faltered as she reached the next chapter of her story. *"And then, things took a turn. My mother developed cancer. There was no one to take care of her back in India. I had to leave my high-profile job and return. It was one of the hardest decisions I've ever made."* Rahul watched her closely as she spoke. The pain of those memories was evident in her eyes.

"Raj followed me back to India. He couldn't bear the thought of me managing everything alone. We had to give up our U.S. citizenship and adopt Indian citizenship. It was a challenging time, with constant running around to take care of ailing elders at home while also managing the needs of small children. The treatment took time, and then, one after another, the elders in the family fell ill. Life turned into a cycle of hospital visits, caregiving, and raising our children, Nikhil and Nikita. Schooling, responsibilities — it felt endless." Simran paused, staring into the distance as if reliving those moments. *"Just when it seemed like life was finally settling down, Raj had a heart attack. He was only forty. There was no warning, no history of illness. He was gone in an instant."* Rahul could sense the weight of her grief, even as she spoke with a composed demeanour.

"Suddenly, everything fell on me. I had to be strong, for our children and for the two families Raj and I were caring for. Nikhil, my elder son, worked hard and became an IAS officer. He's now posted in Benaras. Nikita, my younger daughter, became a doctor and is happily settled in Mumbai with her husband, as mentioned earlier " Simran's voice softened as she concluded, *"Now, I live with Nikhil and my daughter-in-law in Benaras. I teach part-time at BHU. Life isn't what I imagined it would be, but it's steady now."*

Rahul sat quietly, absorbing her story. Simran's journey was one of immense resilience, marked by love, loss, and unwavering strength. For a moment, the restaurant around them seemed to fade away, leaving only the echo of her words lingering between them.

It was almost 2:30 in the afternoon. Neither Rahul nor Simran realised how quickly time had passed. Their conversation had drawn them into a shared bubble, where the outside world seemed distant. Suddenly, Rahul's phone buzzed. It was a call from his friends, checking on him and asking about his plans.

With a warm chuckle, Rahul replied, *"I'm busy at the moment. You all go ahead with the sightseeing as planned. I'll catch up with you later."*

As he ended the call, Simran leaned forward, a curious smile playing on her lips. *"Rahul, enough about me. Now, tell me about yourself."* Rahul hesitated for a moment, his gaze meeting hers. "Simran, I think there's still more to your story, more than you've shared," he said softly. "But let's save that for another time. For now, I'll tell you about my life."

Taking a sip of water, Rahul began, his tone calm but laced with a hint of pride as he recounted his life journey. *"After graduating from school, I decided to pursue a degree in commerce. I worked hard, balancing my studies with part-time jobs to ease the financial burden on my family. Once I completed my graduation, I realised I wanted to push myself further, so I enrolled in an MBA programme. Those two years were intense but rewarding, and I also managed to complete a Law degree alongside it. It wasn't easy, but I knew it would open up doors for me in the corporate world."* I landed in a good job at an MNC and worked there for almost two decades. But eventually, I ventured out on my own and became an entrepreneur."

For the past 12 years, I have been successfully managing and growing my real estate business, transforming it into a thriving enterprise. Over the years, I have built a reputation for integrity, professionalism, and delivering value to my clients. From residential properties to commercial ventures, I've overseen numerous projects that cater to diverse needs, ensuring customer satisfaction remains at the heart of my operations.

Through hard work and a keen understanding of market trends, I have not only expanded my portfolio but also cultivated strong relationships with clients, investors, and industry peers. This journey has been as much about personal growth as it has been about business success, teaching me resilience, adaptability, and the importance of forging trust in every transaction.

THE REVELATION – THE SILENT CONFESSION

He paused, his voice becoming quieter as he continued. *"I don't know if I should tell you this or not, but my life was turned upside down when we left school. I couldn't trace you, Simran."*

I didn't have your address or any way to find you. And the truth is, I loved you deeply but never said a word. Back then, we were all so afraid of losing friendships if we revealed how we felt."

Simran's eyes widened, her expression a mixture of surprise and something unreadable. Rahul pressed on, his tone reflective. *"During my college days, I tried everything to find you."*

I searched and asked around, but nothing worked."

After Rahul's heartfelt revelation about his schoolboy crush on Simran, an air of wistfulness and quiet contemplation enveloped the moment. Simran, caught off guard by the unexpected confession, felt a flicker of warmth rise within her.

She leaned back slightly, letting the serene ambiance of the Ganges fill the silence between them. Her mind wandered back to the corridors of their school — the laughter, the shared glances, and the innocence of youth. She wondered if, somewhere in those fleeting moments, she had unknowingly harboured a similar fondness for Rahul. Her lips curved into a subtle smile, one that danced between curiosity and coyness.

It wasn't a smile that gave away anything concrete; instead, it carried an air of intrigue, as if she were savouring a secret she wasn't ready to share — or perhaps one she herself wasn't entirely sure of.

Rahul, noticing the smile but unable to decipher its meaning, smiled nervously and told Simran *"That smile — are you laughing at me, or are you remembering something?"*

Simran tilted her head slightly, her eyes sparkling with playful mischief. *"Well,"* she began, her tone deliberately teasing, *"let's just say... you're not the only one who remembers those days fondly."* She left it at that, allowing the ambiguity to linger like a wisp of mist over the river. Rahul, both amused and curious, leaned forward. *"That's all you're giving me. No details, no confessions?"*

Simran laughed softly, her voice carrying a note of mystery. *"Some things are better left unsaid, Rahul. Besides, isn't it more fun to let you wonder?"*

As the two shared a knowing glance, the moment became a reflection of their shared history — one filled with unspoken emotions, unanswered questions, and the beauty of rediscovery. The smile on Simran's face wasn't just an expression; it was a gateway to a chapter of her life she hadn't revisited in years, one that now seemed more alive than ever.

Simran asked, *"Rahul, tell me — how did you meet your wife? What's the story behind your marriage? I'd love to hear all about it."* Rahul stated, *"After my MBA, my parents introduced me to a wonderful girl, and we got married. She was from Mumbai, educated, and turned out to be not just a wife but a good friend and partner."*

He smiled faintly, recalling those early days. *"She gave me two amazing sons. Life was good, but every single day, a part of me missed you. I even told her before our engagement that I had feelings for someone back in school. She laughed it off, calling it infatuation."* Simran listened intently, her expression softening as Rahul opened up further.

"My wife hails from a business family. She always encouraged me to start something of my own, and eventually, I did. As mentioned earlier, I launched a real estate venture, and for the last 12 years, it's been going well."

Rahul's voice grew sombre. *"But five years ago, life threw me a curveball. My wife developed a severe ulcer in her uterus. Despite all efforts, we lost her. It's a wound that hasn't healed, but I find solace in my sons. They've joined me in the business, and they're doing well. Because of them, I have the freedom to travel now and take time for myself."*

He leaned back, his eyes resting on Simran. *"That's my story, Simran. Not as turbulent as yours, but with its own share of struggles and losses. And here we are now, after all these years."*

Simran remained silent for a moment, absorbing his words. Her gaze held his, filled with a mixture of empathy, understanding, and perhaps a flicker of something deeper that neither dared to name.

It was almost 5:00 p.m. and the two of them were still immersed in conversation, having finished three cups of coffee each without any sign of leaving. The outside world seemed irrelevant, as if time itself had paused for them.

Suddenly, Simran's phone rang. It was her son.

She casually answered, *"I'll be home late. Don't wait for me for dinner."* After hanging up, she looked at Rahul with a spark in her eyes. *"Let's go for a boat ride,"* she suggested.

The Dashashwamedh Ghat and Ganga Aarti

Rahul, pleasantly surprised, nodded in agreement. They stepped out and hailed an e-auto to head towards the Dashashwamedh Ghat. On the way, Simran asked him, *"Would you like to attend the Ganga Aarti?"* Without hesitation, Rahul smiled and replied, *"Of course."*

Dashashwamedh Ghat

Rahul had planned with his friends to visit the Kashi Vishwanath Temple, take a boat ride on the Ganges, and witness the Ganga Aarti. But destiny, it seemed, had other plans for him – plans that included Simran.

Upon reaching the Ghat, Simran exchanged a few words with a local person, and soon they were boarding a small wooden boat. As the boat pushed away from the shore and glided over the serene waters of the Ganges, a tranquil silence enveloped them. The golden colour of the setting sun reflected on the rippling surface, and the sound of the oars dipping into the water filled the air.

Neither spoke for a while. Rahul was quietly amazed at Simran's composure and balance on the swaying boat, while Simran was still processing Rahul's earlier confession about his feelings during their school days. Breaking the silence, Rahul spoke lightly with a smile, *"Now, tell me about the significance of this Ghat and its history."* Simran, who had been lost in thought, quickly snapped back into action.

Simran began, *"The Ganga Aarti at Dashashwamedh Ghat is a mesmerising and deeply spiritual ritual performed every evening on the banks of the Ganges. This iconic event draws thousands of devotees and tourists from around the world, all coming together to witness the grandeur and devotion of the ceremony."*

She paused, then continued, *"The name 'Dashashwamedh' translates to 'ten horse sacrifices.' According to legend, Lord Brahma, the creator in Hindu mythology, performed ten Ashwamedha Yagnas at this very spot to welcome Lord Shiva to Kashi and establish the city as the holiest of all."* Simran explained further, *"This Ghat is one of the oldest and most revered in Benaras, holding immense spiritual and cultural significance."*

She then turned to Rahul,

"Now, let me tell you about the Ganga Aarti."

"The ceremony begins at sunset, around 6:00–7:00 pm, and lasts for about 45–60 minutes. It is performed by a group of young priests dressed in traditional saffron robes and dhotis. The aarti involves synchronised movements with large brass lamps, incense sticks, conch shells, and the rhythmic chanting of Sanskrit hymns — much like the Ganga Aarti at Assi Ghat. We'll see it once our boat ride is done," Simran mentioned.

"Devotees also light diyas (earthen lamps) and float them on the river as offerings, praying for blessings and purification," she added. Simran's voice softened as she continued, *"In our tradition, the Ganga is considered a goddess, believed to purify the soul and wash away sins. The aarti is an expression of gratitude and reverence for the river, which sustains life and provides spiritual sanctity."*

She paused for a moment before concluding,

"The Dashashwamedh Ghat Ganga Aarti is not just a ritual – it's a soulful celebration of faith, tradition, and the timeless bond between humanity and the sacred Ganga. It's an essential experience for anyone visiting Varanasi." Rahul smiled warmly at her explanation but then changed the topic. With a playful tone, he asked, *"Simran, do you remember that drawing course we took together in school?"*

She turned to him, nodding with a smile. *"Of course, I do."*

Rahul chuckled and said *"That was when we really started getting to know each other. Those three years were some of the best years of my life."*

Simran's expression softened, and a faint smile touched her lips. *"I remember,"*

"And what about our tenth-standard school picnic?" Rahul continued in a light tone. *"The boys and girls were on separate buses, but the girls insisted on mixing up the seating. The boys stayed quiet, but you all were so determined!"*

Simran laughed softly, the memory vivid in her mind.

"I remember that too," she said with a smile.

Despite the light-hearted conversation, Rahul noticed Simran's gaze seemed distant, as though lost in thought. He gently asked, *"What are you thinking?"*

She looked at him with reflective eyes. *'How time flies,'* she said quietly. *'Everything feels so fresh, as if it just happened a few years ago. But look at us — so many years have passed.'*

They spent the next few moments reminiscing about their school days — the breaks, the annual events, the sports meets — sharing smiles that spoke of cherished memories, enjoying the boat ride.

Simran, as their local guide, intertwined their conversation with stories about the ghats they were passing. She told him about Harishchandra Ghat, named after King Harishchandra, who gave up his kingdom to work at the burial ground, and

Manikarnika Ghat, known as a sacred gateway to heaven. By the time their boat returned to Dashashwamedh Ghat, the sky had darkened, and the golden lamps of the ghats glowed against the night, casting a divine light on the river. Rahul turned to Simran. *"I'd love to try some kulhad chai. Would you join me?"*

Simran hesitated for a moment before smiling. *"I've never had tea before,"* she admitted, *"but today, I'll give it a shot."* They went to a nearby tea stall and sipped steaming chai in earthen cups. The rich, earthy aroma mixed perfectly with the cool winter evening. *"This is the best tea I've ever had,"*, Rahul said, his eyes lighting up. Simran laughed. *"You're being too generous,"* she replied, as they made their way back to their reserved seats to watch the Ganga Aarti.

Ganga Maa ki Aarti

The Aarti was nothing short of breathtaking. The lamps swayed in unison, chants filled the air, and the fragrance of incense enveloped the surroundings. Rahul felt an overwhelming sense of peace, and sharing the sacred moment with Simran made it all the more special. He silently thanked the universe for this unforgettable day.

By 7:15 p.m., the Aarti concluded. The spectacle of the giant flames, the scent of incense, the sound of bells, Damru (double-headed drum) and chants, and the reflections of the lights on the Ganga created an ambiance that would forever stay etched in their memories.

Simran added, *"The Ganga Aarti is even more magnificent during festivals like Dev Deepawali, Makar Sankranti, and Kartik Purnima, when the ghats are illuminated with countless diyas and vibrant decorations."* Rahul nodded, a wistful smile crossing his face as he took a moment to collect his thoughts.

Twilight in Benaras –
The Late Evening on Streets of Benaras

The city was cloaked in darkness, the ghats bustling with devotees and tourists. Simran turned to Rahul. *"Would you like to try some of Banaras' Street food?"* Rahul hesitated, concern evident on his face. *"Simran, you've been out with me all day. Don't you need to head home? We can do this tomorrow if you'd like."*

She smiled reassuringly. *"Don't worry about me. I've already told my family I'll be late. Besides, I'm enjoying this day too much to end it just yet."* Her words were enough to ease Rahul's worries, and together, they began exploring the vibrant streets of Banaras, their connection deepening with every shared moment.

As they strolled along the bustling streets of Banaras, the golden glow of the city lights reflecting off the Ganges, Rahul turned to Simran with a soft smile and said, *"You know, we have just 36 hours."* Simran stopped for a moment, looking at him with a curious expression. *"Thirty-six hours?"* she echoed.

"Yes," Rahul replied, his voice calm yet tinged with a sense of urgency. *"I mean, time is fleeting, and we*

only have these two days to catch up on years we've lost. It feels like so much to say, so much to ask... but so little time." Simran's expression softened, and a faint smile curved her lips. *"Thirty-six hours or thirty-six years, Rahul. What matters is how we spend the time we do have. Don't you think?"*

Rahul nodded, his gaze lingering on her. *"You're right, but it's not just about the past, Simran. It's also about the present... and the future."*

Her eyes flickered with a mix of emotions: curiosity and a hint of uncertainty. *"The present is here, Rahul. And we're living it. Let's not worry about the rest, at least not tonight."* An important lesson from Simran.

They continued walking, the lively sounds of the city wrapping around them. Vendors called out, selling piping hot samosas at Mangru stall, jalebis, and chaat. The aroma was irresistible, and Rahul couldn't help but stop at a stall. He gestured to Simran. *"Shall we?"* Simran giggled. *"You're quite the foodie, aren't you?"*

Rahul nodded. *"Maybe. But only because this city has so much to offer. Besides, how can I miss experiencing Benaras through your eyes?"*

Simran shook her head playfully but joined him as they indulged in Spicy Samosas, crispy pani puri, and tangy tamatar chaat. They laughed over Rahul's exaggerated reaction to the spice, their banter light and carefree.

Walking through the narrow, winding streets, they finally reached Panchaganga Ghat, a quieter and more peaceful spot compared to the bustling Assi Ghat or the lively Dashashwamedh Ghat.

PANCHAGANGA GHAT

Simran continued her narration, *"Panchaganga Ghat is one of the city's hidden gems — lesser-known yet deeply significant. It holds both spiritual and historical importance and offers a quieter retreat compared to the bustling Assi Ghat or Dashashwamedh Ghat. The name 'Panchaganga' comes from the belief that five sacred rivers — the Ganga, Yamuna, Saraswati, Kirana, and Dhutpapa — converge here. While some of these rivers have vanished or changed course over time, the belief enhances the Ghat's spiritual appeal, drawing devotees seeking tranquillity and purification.*

Panchaganga Ghat is also renowned for its proximity to the Panchaganga Temple, a revered shrine dedicated to Lord Vishnu. This temple is thought to have been constructed by the Maratha ruler, Chhatrapati Shahu Maharaj, adding a layer of historical depth to the site. Unlike the more crowded ghats of Benaras, Panchaganga Ghat offers a serene and meditative atmosphere. It's an ideal spot for visitors who wish to immerse themselves in the city's spiritual and cultural essence without the usual clamour."

As they sat on a step overlooking the river, the quiet of the night settling around them, Rahul spoke again. *"Simran, these 36 hours may be brief, but being with you has made them feel infinite. It's as if the years we lost are catching up in the best way possible.*" Simran looked at him, her face thoughtful. "*It's strange, isn't it? How life brings people back together when they least expect it. You've had your journey, and I've had mine. But somehow, we're here, sharing this moment.*"

Rahul gazed at her, the weight of unspoken words lingering between them. "*Maybe some things are meant to happen, no matter how much time has passed.*"

The river flowed quietly in the background, its rhythm steady and eternal, mirroring the connection they had rediscovered. As they sat there, neither spoke, yet the silence between them felt profound, as though the Ganges itself was bearing witness to their reunion.

It was 8:30 at night, and time had flown by in a blur of conversations, memories, and shared moments. Rahul looked at Simran, a mix of gratitude and hesitation in his eyes. "*Let me drop you home,*" he offered.

Simran smiled, her eyes sparkling with a mix of warmth and mischief. "*This is my hometown, Rahul. I'll drop you home,*" she teased. "*But I can still spend another hour with you, if you don't mind.*" Rahul's face lit up, a twinkle in his eyes. "*Happily,*" he said without hesitation.

The conversation resumed, flowing effortlessly like a river meandering through old landscapes. Simran leaned back slightly, her gaze turning thoughtful. "*Tell me, Rahul,*" she began. "*You were such a passionate singer in school. Did you ever pursue singing? And if I'm not mistaken, you always loved travelling. Where all have you been?"*

Rahul smiled at the mention of his younger self and replied. *"Singing? Not much. Life took over, you know. But travelling, yes — that's something I've kept alive. My love for it came from my parents. As a family, we explored over 50% of the country by road before my mother passed away."* He paused, a shadow of sorrow briefly crossing his face. *"After her death, my father became deeply spiritual, and our travels stopped. But post-marriage, I picked it up again."*

My wife was a traveller too. We used to take two short vacations and one long vacation every year. In between, there were plenty of road trips. Over time, we've covered most of Europe and Asia. The United States is still on my list," he added with a smile.

Simran listened intently, her focus unwavering. As Rahul recounted his adventures, she seemed lost in her own thoughts. He noticed the distant look in her eyes and gently asked, *"Everything okay?"* Simran shook off the momentary reverie and smiled. *"Yes, everything's fine. It's just that I've barely seen India, let alone the world. I have a long way to go. But your stories are inspiring. Keep going — I'm making mental notes of where I should visit next."*

Rahul thought of something and said it, which brought a smile to Simran's face. *'Don't worry, Simran,'* he said warmly. *If you can spare some time, I'll take you out and plan some wonderful outings regularly.'* With a cheerful smile, Simran replied, *'Yes, I'll wait for that.'* Their laughter mingled with the faint hum of the city as they continued talking, weaving memories and plans together. Before they realised it, the clock struck at 10:00 p.m. Simran called for her driver, who arrived promptly to take her to Rahul's hotel. As the car came to a stop, Rahul asked,

"So, what's the plan for tomorrow?"

"Sarnath," Simran answered without hesitation. *"It's only fifteen kilometres from here. I'll pick you up at 9:00 a.m. sharp — if that's alright?"* she added, seeking confirmation. Rahul responded with a grateful nod. They shook hands, a simple yet significant gesture. *"A day well spent,"* Rahul said, smiling. Simran nodded in agreement before the car drove off.

BANTER WITH FRIENDS

Back in his hotel room, Rahul found his friends waiting eagerly. They bombarded him with questions, their curiosity palpable. *"Ten minutes,"* Rahul said, excusing himself to freshen up.

When he joined them at the hotel's in-house restaurant, he opted for a light soup, citing his indulgence in street food earlier with a mischievous grin. His friends laughed, declaring, *"Good! Now you can focus on sharing your day's adventures instead of eating!"* Rahul tried to divert the topic, asking about their explorations in Benaras instead. They had spent the day ticking off their bucket list, visiting temples, ghats, and shops. As their food arrived, the aroma filled the air, and they dove into their plates with gusto, hardly pausing to talk.

After dinner, someone suggested a drive to find an authentic Banarasi paan. Rahul joined them, but his thoughts remained with Simran. The friends took the opportunity to press him for details. Reluctantly, he narrated his day, condensing hours of emotions into a ten-minute summary.

"What's the plan for tomorrow?" one of them asked as they cruised through the quiet streets.

"BHU for us, and maybe some shopping," another chimed in.

Rahul's answer was simple: *"Sarnath."*

The response was immediate. *"Wow planned another day without us?"* they teased, laughing and nudging him. *"Carry on, bro! Enjoy and tell us everything later."*

The night ended with Banarasi paan, a lingering sweetness on their tongues. But sleep remained elusive for Rahul. Alone in his room, he debated whether to text Simran. What if she thought it was too soon?

Just then, his phone buzzed. It was a message from Simran," *Good night."*

A smile spread across Rahul's face as he quickly typed a response: *"Good night. See you tomorrow."*

But even as he tried to sleep, thoughts of the day — and of Simran — kept him awake, stirring memories and dreams alike.

DAY 2 : THE SARNATH EXPERIENCE

MALAIYO – THE TASTE OF BENARAS

Rahul was ready by 8:45 am, excitement bubbling beneath his calm demeanour. As he waited in the hotel lobby, his thoughts wandered to Simran—her stories, her graceful poise, and the way she effortlessly commanded attention without even trying.

At exactly 9:00, Simran arrived, punctual as always. They greeted each other with a friendly handshake, her warm smile setting the tone for a pleasant day. As they settled into the car, she turned to Rahul and asked, *"Have you had your breakfast?"*

Rahul nodded somewhat bashfully. *"Yes. And you?"*

"I usually have a late breakfast," she replied with a smile.

As the car merged onto the main road, Simran glanced at him and asked, *"Have you heard about Malaiyo?"*

Rahul's face lit up. *"Yes, I've read about it. It's a sweet delicacy made from milk."* Simran's eyes sparkled with enthusiasm. *"Would you like to try it before we head to*

Sarnath? This is the perfect time." Without hesitation, Rahul agreed.

As they drove deeper into the heart of Benaras, Simran began to elaborate. *"Let me tell you more about Malaiyo. It's a beloved winter dessert here, light and frothy, almost like eating a cloud. It's made by boiling milk, flavouring it with saffron and cardamom, and then leaving it out overnight under the winter sky to absorb the dew. That's what gives it its unique, airy texture."* (*Malaiyo Recipe shared at the end of this topic*)

The car soon reached a spot where they parked and began walking through the narrow bylanes of Benaras, alive with morning hustle. Narrow and winding, the lanes lined with old-style homes, intricate wooden doors, and walls adorned with vibrant murals. These lanes tell stories of a bygone era, blending history and daily life.

Simran continued, *"Once the milk is whipped into a cloud-like froth, it's garnished with slivers of pistachios, almonds, and sometimes edible silver leaf. It's served in clay cups, or kulhads, which keep it cool and add a rustic charm."* Rahul listened intently as they navigated the winding streets. He could almost taste the subtle sweetness and creamy flavour she described. *"It's best enjoyed fresh, early in the morning,"*

Simran added." *Vendors sell it in areas like Chowk, Godowlia, and Thatheri Bazaar. And trust me, Malaiyo isn't just a dessert — it's a cultural experience that captures the essence of Varanasi's winter mornings."* Their walk led them to a small stall famous for Malaiyo, bustling with youngsters capturing their moments on camera for social media. The vibrant energy of the place, combined with the rich aroma of saffron and cardamom, made the experience even more inviting. On reaching the stall, Rahul turned to Simran with a smile." *You were right – it's more than just a dessert. I can't wait to try it."*

After savouring the delicate sweetness of Malaiyo, Rahul said

"I had no idea so much went into making it," he confessed.

"It's like creating a piece of art – no wonder it feels so magical to eat," Simran smiled, her excitement spreading to those around her.

"Exactly. You don't just taste Malaiyo; you experience it."

Both Rahul and Simran felt a renewed energy after enjoying Malaiyo.

They exchanged a contented smile as they made their way back through the lively bylanes of Benaras, heading towards the car for their onward journey to Sarnath.

Traditional Recipe of Malaiyo from Benaras

Malaiyo, a winter delicacy from Varanasi, is a light, frothy dessert made from milk, infused with saffron and cardamom, and topped with nuts. It's a time-intensive traditional preparation but worth every effort. Do check the recipe card to prepare it yourself.

INGREDIENTS

- **1 ltr. full-fat milk**
(fresh and unadulterated milk)
- **Pinch of saffron strands**
(soaked in 2 tbsp. of warm milk)
- **3-4 green cardamom pods**
(crushed into powder)
- **Chopped pistachios and almonds**
(for garnishing)

OPTIONAL
- **Edible silver leaf**
(varq) for decoration

DIRECTIONS

1. MILK PREPARATION:

- Boil the milk in a large pan until it slightly reduces and thickens.
- Add the saffron-infused milk and cardamom powder to enhance the flavor.
- Let the milk simmer for a few more minutes, stirring occasionally.

2. COOLING OVERNIGHT:

- Pour the flavored milk into a wide, shallow pan or large bowl.
- Cover it lightly with a thin muslin cloth and leave it outside overnight in a cool, open area.
The natural dew of winter nights helps form the characteristic froth on top.

3. WHIPPING THE FROTH:

- The next morning, gently skim off the frothy layer that forms on the surface and then transfer this froth to a mixing bowl and whisk it thoroughly until it becomes fluffy and airy. Traditionally, this step is done by hand with a wooden whisk (mathani).

4. ADDING SWEETNESS:

- While whisking, slowly fold in the powdered sugar to sweeten the froth without losing its light texture.

5. SERVING AND GARNISHING:

- Spoon the whipped Malaiyo into small earthen bowls (kulhads) or serving dishes.
- Sprinkle chopped pistachios and almonds generously on top.
- Optionally, adorn with a touch of edible silver leaf for an authentic presentation.

SERVING TIPS

- Malaiyo is best enjoyed fresh and chilled. It's incredibly light and dissolves in your mouth, making it a unique dessert experience.
- Pair it with a hot cup of chai or savor it on its own to appreciate its delicate flavors.

PRO TIP

The magic of Malaiyo lies in its environment—winter mornings and the natural dew contribute to its frothy, ethereal texture.
While recreating it at home, ensure the milk is left in a cool, dry place to mimic this effect.

JOURNEY TO SARNATH

The streets were abuzz with morning activity—vendors calling out, the aroma of fresh snacks wafting through the air, and pilgrims moving purposefully toward the ghats. Simran walked with an effortless grace, occasionally pointing out little details of the city's charm—an intricately carved doorway, a quaint shop, or a fleeting moment of local life.

"Malaiyo was incredible," Rahul said, breaking the pleasant silence. *"I can see why it's so iconic here. It's not just the taste but the experience—the ambiance, the morning chill, everything adds to it."*

Simran smiled. *"That's the beauty of Varanasi. Every little thing here, even a dessert, carries a sense of tradition and magic."* *"I told you, Rahul, in Benaras, even something as simple as a dessert tells a story."*

Reaching the car, they settled into their seats, the city slowly giving way to quieter roads as they left behind the vibrant chaos of Varanasi. Rahul, glancing out the window, felt a quiet anticipation for Sarnath, where history, spirituality, and calm awaited. *"You'll love Sarnath,"* Simran said, as if reading his thoughts. *"It's so serene and holds such a profound sense of history. The energy there is completely different.*

"Do you know anything about Sarnath?" asked Simran *"Not much,"* Rahul admitted. *"I only know it's a Buddhist place."* Simran inquired. *"Would you like me to tell you more?"*

"Of course," he replied eagerly. Simran began, her voice steady yet brimming with reverence. *"Sarnath is not just a place — it's a symbol of transformation and enlightenment. It's where Gautama Buddha gave his first sermon after attaining enlightenment."*

This event is called the Dhammacakkappavattana Sutta, or 'Setting in Motion the Wheel of Dharma.' It was here that the Buddhist Sangha, the monastic community, was born."

Rahul listened intently as she continued. *"During the Mauryan Empire, Emperor Ashoka made Sarnath a centre of learning and pilgrimage. He erected the Ashoka Pillar, which bears inscriptions promoting non-violence and dharma. Its lion capital now serves as India's national emblem."*

She described the main attractions with a storyteller's finesse:

"The Dhamek Stupa, marking the spot of Buddha's first sermon, is a masterpiece of ancient architecture. The Chaukhandi Stupa commemorates Buddha's meeting with his first disciples."

"The Sarnath Museum houses relics, including the original lion capital of Ashoka's Pillar."

"Temples and monasteries, built by countries like Japan, Tibet, and Thailand, each showcasing unique architectural styles."

She concluded, *"Sarnath is a place where history, spirituality, and peace converge. We'll explore all of this today."* Rahul smiled. *"The way you described it; I feel like I've already seen it!"*

Simran laughed softly. *"Wait until we actually get there. Ten more minutes."* Rahul suddenly remembered she hadn't eaten and asked, *"How about we stop somewhere for breakfast?"*

She hesitated but finally suggested a vegetarian restaurant near Sarnath Chauraha. They soon arrived, and as they settled at a corner table, Rahul saw his chance to steer the conversation back to her.

Conversations Over Breakfast

"Let's pick up where we left off yesterday at Ganges," Rahul said, his tone playful yet sincere.

Simran raised an eyebrow, feigning innocence. *'What do you mean?'*

"Your story," he clarified. *"That's why I'm here — to reconnect and catch up on everything we missed over the years. I can see Sarnath through your eyes, but being with you is what matters most."*

Simran gave a small, knowing smile. *"Alright. But only if you share more about your singing first. I still remember you singing 'Main Shayar To Nahi' from 'Bobby' during our 10th standard annual day, and 'Dil Kya Kare' from 'Julie' the year before. You were quite the star back then."* Rahul's eyes widened in disbelief. *"You remember that after all these years?"*

"Of course," she replied with a soft smile. *"You had a lot of fans, you know. Especially among the girls in our class."*

Rahul blushed, shaking his head. *"It was nothing serious. Singing was just a passion. I wanted to learn classical music, but life had other plans. I mostly sang at gatherings with friends. But now, with more free time, I've been thinking about taking it up seriously."* Simran leaned forward, with interest. *"Tell me more. Any memorable singing moments?"*

Rahul smiled, reminiscing. *"One memory that stands out is from a family trip to Nainital about 20 years ago. The resort we were staying at hosted a karaoke night. I mentioned that I wanted to join in and sing, but my wife and kids tried to talk me out of it, saying I'd embarrass them. They didn't even know I could sing!"*

Simran laughed. *"And did you?"*

"Quite the opposite," Rahul said proudly. *"I sang Main Shayar To Nahi, and the crowd loved it. My wife was shocked, and my boys couldn't believe their ears. Since then, my wife used to request me to sing whenever we had free time. It became our little thing."*

He paused, his smile softening. *"It's nothing extraordinary, but it's always been fun. That's my singing story."* Simran listened with rapt attention, her expression a blend of admiration and *"You should definitely pursue it now."*

"Well, enough about me," Rahul said, leaning back. *"Your turn."* Simran hesitated, looking out the window for a moment before turning back to him. *"Alright. Let's talk about me."*

And so, over a leisurely breakfast, the threads of their pasts and present began to weave a tapestry of shared memories and newfound understanding, setting the stage for another unforgettable day.

Simran's voice carried a soft yearning as she shared her love for swimming and badminton. *"Swimming was my first love,"* she said, her eyes twinkling with pride. *"I started when I was barely two or three years old. My father was a professional swimmer and taught me himself. By the time I was in college, I was competing at the state and national levels, even representing Mumbai in competitive swimming."*

Rahul leaned forward, visibly impressed. *"That's incredible, Simran! Competitive swimming and academics — how did you balance it all?"*

She shrugged modestly. *"Swimming felt natural to me. It wasn't something I had to force myself to do. It came effortlessly, and I loved it. My favourite was sea swimming - covering twenty-five kilometres at a stretch!"* *"Twenty-five kilometres?"* Rahul exclaimed. *"That's more than remarkable — it's heroic!"*

Simran smiled softly, brushing off his praise. *"But all of that stopped when I moved to the US. Life changed; priorities shifted. I still kept active, though. I took up badminton at the club level and later pursued piano lessons."*

"Piano?" Rahul asked, his curiosity piqued.

"Yes," she replied, her smile widening. *"When my children started singing lessons, I had to wait during their classes. So, I joined the same institute to learn the piano. It turned out to be a wonderful decision. I play quite well now."* She paused, then added with a laugh, *"You sing, I'll play the piano. We'd make a good duo!"*

Rahul laughed heartily. *"We could even start our own music company,"* he joked.

Simran nodded with a light laugh but added seriously, *"My son is a trained singer too. He's the best among all the IAS officers, I'd say."*

Their conversation ebbed and flowed like the Ganges, warm and easy. As they sipped the last of their tea, Simran glanced at her watch. *"It's noon already. Let's head to the Buddhist temple."*

SARNATH AND BEYOND

The Buddhist temple stood as a tranquil sanctuary amidst the bustling world. Its serene surroundings and meditative aura seemed to calm their spirits instantly. Simran moved through the space with reverence, her demeanour reflecting her deep connection to the place.

Rahul, intrigued, asked, *"Do you come here often?"*

"Yes," she said with a gentle smile. *"Whenever I can, I visit. Sarnath is where I find my peace. It's perfect for meditation and reflection."*

As they moved from one site to another, their conversations continued, each question peeling back more layers of their shared and separate histories. Simran then asked if their school had ever organised a reunion, picnics, and if Rahul was in touch with their classmates.

"Thanks to technology, yes," Rahul replied. *"We have a school alumni group on WhatsApp and Facebook. I can add you if you'd like."*

Simran hesitated, her expression thoughtful. *"Let's wait. I'll decide after meeting everyone."*

Curious, she asked who all were part of the group. Rahul pulled out his phone and read through the list, watching as recognition flickered across her face, she said with excitement, *"I remember most of them,"* *"The next time I visit Mumbai, I'd love to reconnect with everyone."*

Their conversation had moved from formal to personal, with the gap of 40 years fading away as the moments passed.

Sarnath's Historic Landmarks

They visited the Dhamek Stupa, where Buddha delivered his first sermon, and the Chaukhandi Stupa, commemorating his meeting with his first disciples. The sheer history embedded in these sites left Rahul in awe.

At the Sarnath Museum, he admired the original lion capital of Ashoka's Pillar and other ancient relics. Standing before the towering 84-foot statue of Gautama Buddha, Simran spoke with quiet reverence. *"Temples and monasteries here reflect the devotion of countries like Japan, Tibet, and Thailand. Each one is unique, yet all are bound by the same thread of spirituality."*

Dhamek Stupa

Buddha Statue at Sarnath

Rahul listened, his respect for Simran deepening. Her knowledge, grace, and passion for these places were inspiring.

Ashoka Pillar at Sarnath

A Day to Remember

By the time their exploration of Sarnath drew to a close, the sun began its descent, painting the ancient site in shades of gold and amber. The fading light bathed the ruins in a serene glow, adding a sense of quiet reverence to the atmosphere. The day had been an immersive journey through history, spirituality, and personal reflection, and both Rahul and Simran carried a sense of contentment in their hearts.

As they returned to the car, a comfortable silence lingered between them, broken only by the occasional rustling of leaves and the distant sound of temple bells. It was a silence that spoke volumes — of understanding, shared moments, and an unspoken connection rekindled after decades.

Rahul broke the silence, turning to Simran with a smile equal to gratitude and admiration. *"Thank you for today,"* he said earnestly. *"Not just for being a wonderful guide, but for sharing so much of yourself — your thoughts, memories, and world. It's been a gift."*

Simran paused, her expression softening as she met his gaze. *"And thank you,"* she replied, her voice tinged with warmth. *"For being such a good listener.*

It's not often you find someone who genuinely cares to hear your story, who listens without judgement or distraction."

The words hung in the air, their mutual appreciation deepening the bond that had grown over the day. There was no need for grand gestures or elaborate conversations. This simple exchange was enough to solidify what they had rediscovered in each other: a sense of comfort, trust, and a connection that transcended time.

As they drove back towards the heart of Benaras, the radiant tones of the setting sun reflected the warmth radiating within their hearts. Much like the city around them, the day had been timeless—a reminder of how even fleeting moments could leave a lasting imprint on the soul.

As the Clock Winds Down – Cherishing the Last Few Hours

The car moved steadily through the streets of Sarnath, heading back to Benaras. Rahul gazed out the window, his thoughts weaving between the moments they had spent together over the past two days. Clearing his throat and breaking the silence, he spoke softly, almost as if reluctant to disturb the moment's harmony. *"We only have a few hours left today,"* he said, his voice tinged with the faintest trace of melancholy.

Simran turned to him, her eyes glinting with understanding. *"Yes, we do,"* she repeated, her tone light yet comforting. *"But remember, Rahul, there's always tomorrow – and the day after."*

Rahul glanced at her, his brows lifting in question. She laughed, her voice carrying a warmth that filled the small space of the car. *"Yes, tomorrow you'll leave Benaras,"* she said with a knowing smile. *"But that doesn't mean we won't be available to each other. Distance doesn't have to matter, does it?"*

Rahul couldn't help but smile at her optimism, but she wasn't finished.

"*Let's not focus on the hours slipping away,*" Simran continued. "*Instead, let's make these hours count. Let's do something that makes this day unforgettable — not because it's our last, but because we chose to make it meaningful.*" One more wisdom capsule from Simran. Simran continued, "*We are all tourists, and life has already mapped out our routes, bookings, and destinations. Trust the Journey and enjoy every moment*"

Her words carried a weight that settled gently on Rahul's heart. He nodded, her positivity lifting the cloud of impending goodbyes. "*You're right,*" he said, his voice steady now. "*Let's make today a memory worth keeping.*"

As they drove back, the silence between them was comfortable, filled with the unspoken understanding that this reunion was as much about rediscovery as it was about the moments they were creating now.

REFLECTIONS AT KEDAR GHAT

As the sun set, casting the sky in shades of orange and pink, Simran proposed they spend their last hours of the day at the ghats. They opted for a more peaceful spot, Kedar Ghat, away from the crowds and commotion. Before them, the Ganges lay calm, mirroring the vibrant colours of the sunset, its waters gleaming like liquid gold.

Kedar Ghat, situated on the southern banks of the Ganges River in Benaras, is one of the city's many revered ghats. It holds profound religious significance, especially for Hindus who seek spiritual purification through the Ganges. The Ghat is named after the Kedarnath Temple in Uttarakhand and is dedicated to Lord Shiva.

The host, Simran, started, *"Rahul, let me tell you the key points about this Ghat." "Like other ghats in Benaras, Kedar Ghat is a vital location for bathing and performing religious rituals, particularly for those searching for salvation (moksha)."*

"Pilgrims believe bathing in the Ganges here helps cleanse them of their sins."

"Nearby, there is a small temple dedicated to Lord Shiva, which adds to its significance as a place of worship."

"At this Ghat, devotees and locals also gather for daily rituals, such as pujas (prayers) and cremation ceremonies, which are an integral part of Varanasi's spiritual atmosphere."

Overall, Kedar Ghat offers a quiet, serene spot for reflection and is deeply rooted in Varanasi's religious and cultural fabric.

They sat on the cool stone steps, their shoulders nearly brushing, both lost in their own reverie.

The distant chants of the evening aarti mixed with the soft rustle of the river's flow, creating a tranquil harmony that seemed to hold them in its embrace.

Simran spoke, her voice cutting through the stillness. *"Rahul, I've been wondering how quickly time has flown. Sitting here, chatting with you, it feels like we're back in school. In reality, it's been decades. It's funny, isn't it? Age is truly just a number."*

Rahul smiled, his eyes fixed on the river. *"It does feel that way. And you're right — time seems to vanish when you're with old friends. When I meet our schoolmates, we talk about how nothing has changed. We laugh, share stories, and suddenly back in those corridors again."*

Simran's curiosity was piqued. *'You all still meet often? What's that like?'*

Rahul smiled, *"We do, at least two or three times a year."*

But thanks to WhatsApp, it feels like we meet every day! Some of our teachers are also in touch, and we invite them whenever we have reunions. It's like a big family.

Birthdays, anniversaries, weddings, achievements — we celebrate everything together. Some of our friends who've moved abroad join us when they visit. We take extra efforts to make that special meeting happen. And those of us who live nearby, we meet for breakfast or dinner regularly. It's refreshing — it keeps us young."

Simran smiled wistfully. "You're lucky to have that."

She paused as if debating something in her mind. Then, with a playful grin, she said, *"I have so many questions in my mind — you might think Simran is being silly."*

Rahul shook his head and interrupted her gently. *"Simran, this is what friendship is. You can be as silly as you like without judgement. That's the beauty of it."*

Her smile widened. *"It's only been two days since we met, after four decades, but it doesn't feel that way. I feel like I was just in school with you yesterday."*

"Tell me," Rahul urged, *"what's on your mind?"*

Kedar Ghat

REMINISCING THE SCHOOL TALK

Simran leaned back slightly, her tone growing playful. *"Shall I tell you some school secrets?"*

"Please do," Rahul replied with an eager grin.

Simran began with a laugh, *"Well, we girls were definitely ahead of you boys in every way. During the school's annual exhibitions, we'd make clever excuses and sneak off to watch movies during school hours. And you guys? You'd be clueless, wondering where we disappeared!"*

Rahul laughed loudly. *"And you thought you could fool us? We were well aware of the girls' intent and reputation."*

Simran's tone turned playful, a glint of mischief in her eyes. *"You know,"* she began, *"back then, every girl had someone she secretly admired — it was all just in their head, of course."* Then, teasingly, she added, *"And guess what? You were definitely on their hit list."*

Rahul's eyes sparkled with equal mischief as he leaned in slightly. *"Oh really?"* he said playfully. *"Now you have to tell me — who all had me on their hit list?"*

Simran, skillfully dodging the question. *"No point going back now, Rahul,"* she said with a playful shrug. Then, tilting her head curiously, she added, *"Tell me, was there any school love story you know of that actually turned into a happily-ever-after?"*

Rahul smiled. *"Not many; a couple of lovebirds managed to turn their school romance into marriage. They're still together and very active in our alumni group. Once you come to Mumbai, you'll meet them. They have some amazing stories to share."*

Simran tilted her head thoughtfully. *"What about you guys? Were you all as unaware as we assumed?"*

Rahul laughed again. *"Oh, most of us were, I admit. But we did have a few mischief-makers in the group. Remember the incident? Those boys brought a smoke bomb to the washroom and caused chaos in the entire school!"*

Simran's eyes lit up. *"I remember! I can't believe they got away with that."*

"They're successful businessmen now," Rahul said with a smile.

"It's incredible to see how far everyone has come. Life has a way of surprising us." Their conversation flowed effortlessly, weaving between the past and the present. Simran's posture had changed—she was more at ease, her movements relaxed, and her words carried a personal warmth. It felt as though the barriers of time and distance had dissolved entirely.

They sat in silence for a while, their hearts full, as the day gave way to the night. The Ganges continued its eternal flow, bearing witness to their timeless bond. Simran smirked and said, *"Some time for my entertainment,"* looked up and asked, *"Rahul, can I get to listen to some songs? It's been such a long time."*

Rahul hesitated, *"We really shouldn't waste any time,"* he began, but the hopeful look in her eyes softened his resolve. He sighed and relented. *"Alright, fine. Which song do you want me to sing?"*

A playful smile danced on Simran's lips. *"Sing the Julie song,"* she said without missing a beat.

Rahul raised an eyebrow, a teasing grin forming. *"The Julie song? That old classic? You're testing my vocal skills here."*

Simran laughed, her voice light and melodic. *"Come on, Rahul. I know you'll do great. Besides, it's one of my favourites."*

He shook his head, chuckling as he cleared his throat.

Rahul started playing Tanpura on his Sur Sadhak App and began with a soft hum. His voice was tentative at first, but as the tune flowed, he gained control. His deep voice carried the melody, filling the space between them. Simran closed her eyes, letting the familiar notes wash over her, her body gently swaying to the rhythm.

When the song ended, a stillness hung in the air. Simran opened her eyes and expressed, *"This song,"* she said softly, *"takes me back to simpler times when everything seemed possible."* Rahul studied her, his gaze steady. *"Do you miss those times?"*

"Sometimes," she admitted, a wistful smile touching her lips. *"But moments like this make me realise those feelings aren't lost. They're still there, waiting to be*

rediscovered." Another wisdom capsule. Rahul nodded thoughtfully. *"If singing a song can bring that out in you, I'd say it's worth it. Feel free to make more requests."*

Simran laughed, a carefree sound that seemed to lighten the air. *"Be careful, Rahul. I might just take you up on that offer."* *I would like to hear more songs from your playlist.*

Rahul opened his notes on the phone to choose the songs and began singing a few heartfelt songs for Simran, unplugged. Simran was completely captivated as his voice filled the air, losing herself in the melody. When Rahul finished his final song, a serene silence enveloped them, broken only by the gentle murmur of the Ganges flowing nearby.

For a while, they sat together in silence, the echoes of the song lingering between them like an unspoken promise.

"Simran," Rahul began once again, his voice warm with gratitude, *"Thank you for today — for showing me Sarnath, being such a fantastic guide, and sharing all the details meticulously. But most of all, thank you for reminding me how beautiful connections can remain, even after all these years."*

She turned to him, her expression soft. *"Rahul, life is made of moments like these. It's not about how long we've known someone or how much time we have left. It's about the depth of the connection we share. And this — what we have — it's special."* Another wisdom capsule.

Rahul nodded, her words resonating deeply. They sat there in comfortable silence, the moment stretching infinitely as if the universe itself wanted to hold on to their fleeting time together.

PARTING MOMENTS

As the night deepened, they walked back to the car. Simran looked at him with a teasing smile. *"So, what's the plan for tomorrow?"*

Shaking his head, Rahul said, *"You tell me, Simran. You are the best planner here."*

Simran paused for a moment, her eyes reflecting anticipation. *"How about we have breakfast together before you leave? A quiet morning to wrap up our time in Benaras."* Rahul's face lit up. *"That sounds perfect."*

She hesitated briefly, then added with a warm smile, *"Also, if you're okay with it, we could meet earlier to experience Subah-e-Banaras — the sunrise by the Ganges. It's magical, truly one of a kind. For that, we'd need to meet around 5:30 a.m."* Rahul's face broke into a complete, radiant smile.

The idea of witnessing the ethereal beauty of Benaras at dawn, alongside Simran, felt like the perfect way to conclude this unexpected journey. *"I'd love that,"* he said earnestly. "Subah-e-Banaras it is."

Simran nodded, pleased. *"Great. Let's meet at Assi Ghat. We can take a boat ride and enjoy the morning prayers, music, and the serenity of the river before breakfast."*

Rahul couldn't help but feel a pang of sadness as he thought about their fleeting time together. But he quickly pushed the thought aside, deciding instead to savour every moment of their last morning in the city that had brought them together after so many years.

Simran's calm yet vibrant energy grounded him, making him feel like time stood still whenever they were together.

"*Alright,*" he said with a deep breath, "*I'll be there at 5:30. Let's make it a morning to remember.*"

And with that, their plan for a memorable farewell to Benaras was set.

As they parted ways for the evening, the weight of the impending goodbye hung lightly in the air, softened by the promise of one last morning together.

THE FINAL EVENING

Rahul reached the hotel at 8:30 p.m., where his friends were eagerly waiting — not for dinner but to hear about his day. His adventure intrigued them: a traveller lost in conversation with an old friend.

As they chatted, a friend asked, *"What's the plan for dinner, Rahul?"* Rahul replied confidently, *"Of course, I'll have dinner today."* His friends teased him, *"Didn't you take your friend out for dinner?"* Smiling humbly, Rahul said, *"We were so absorbed in our conversation that we forgot about dinner entirely."*

Feeling a pang of guilt, Rahul quickly picked up his phone and messaged Simran, apologising for not asking her to join him for dinner. Just as he sent the message, he received one from Simran, apologising for the same. As he read her words, a peaceful smile spread across his face — it seemed their bond grew even deeper through the shared lapse.

Later, the group headed out to a nearby place they had carefully researched — an eatery named *Baati Chokha*. They were eager to try the local delicacy of Benaras.

The Baati Chokha Restaurant

Baati Chokha is a traditional and cherished dish from the region. It's a hearty meal comprising two main elements:

Baati: Round dough balls made from wheat flour, stuffed with a spiced mixture of roasted gram flour (*sattu*) and baked over coal or cow dung cakes for a unique, smoky flavour.

Chokha: A flavoursome mash of roasted eggplant, tomatoes, and boiled potatoes, seasoned with spices and mustard oil.

Together, *Baati* and *Chokha* create a wholesome and satisfying meal. The dish is a staple in local homes and a popular street food in Banaras, often served with pickles, chutneys, and salads. The rustic setting of the eateries enhances the experience, offering an authentic taste of the region's rich culinary traditions. At the restaurant, the group enjoyed a distinctive dining experience. The buttermilk was served in earthen pots, and the food was presented on leaves placed over wooden plates. The simplicity and earthy flavours transported them into the heart of Benaras's cultural essence.

During dinner, Rahul's friends could not hide their curiosity. They bombarded him with playful questions about his day, teasingly suggesting that he might soon leave everything behind and migrate to Benaras. Their laughter echoed in the room, adding warmth to the evening.

With his characteristic simplicity, Rahul recounted his day. He spoke about his serene visit to Sarnath, his tranquil evening spent at Kedar Ghat, and the plan for the next day—an early morning experience of Subah-e-Benaras followed by a hearty breakfast. Each word was laced with the quiet excitement of someone truly embracing the city's spirit.

Yet, his friends were not entirely satisfied. They leaned in, urging him to share more details, their curiosity unquenched. But Rahul, ever composed, responded with nothing more than a soft, knowing smile. That smile spoke volumes, as if saying some experiences are too personal or profound to be fully expressed in words. It left his friends intrigued and a little envious of the connection he had forged with the magical city of Benaras.

For Rahul, the day concluded on a note of pure contentment—a hearty meal shared with friends, heartfelt conversations with Simran that rekindled an old bond, and the quiet joy of immersing himself in the vibrant yet soulful essence of Benaras. It wasn't just a day spent; it was a day lived fully, leaving him with memories to treasure and a deep appreciation for the city's timeless charm.

DAY 3 : FAREWELL MOMENTS

Last Morning with Simran – "Subah-e-Banaras"

The morning air carried a cool crispness, a gentle reminder that it was his final day in Benaras. Rahul stood in the hotel lobby, waiting for the electric auto to take him to the meeting spot. His thoughts were a mix of emotions—gratitude for the memories created and a hint of sadness, knowing his time in this magical city was drawing to a close.

By 5:20 a.m., he reached the Kashi Tea Café, the agreed-upon rendezvous point. The dim glow of streetlights cast a soft, golden hue, and the city seemed to hum with an early morning stillness.

At precisely 5:30 a.m., Simran arrived, her silhouette framed by the faint light of dawn. She carried an effortless grace, her warm smile radiating a quiet energy that perfectly matched the tranquil morning. *"Right on time,"* she said, her voice light and cheerful.

Rahul smiled back. *"Couldn't miss this for the world."*

And so, together, they stepped into the unfolding day, ready to embrace the magic of Subah-e-Banaras.

Simran's suggestion lingered in Rahul's mind as they walked along the ghats of the Ganges. *"Subah-e-Banaras,"* she had called it, describing the magic of the mornings in this ancient city. And now, standing amidst the unfolding beauty, Rahul understood precisely what she meant.

Soft strains of classical Indian music filled the air, played by musicians at Assi Ghat. Their melodies wove into the morning soundscape, mingling with the gentle murmur of the river. The sky transformed into a canvas of gold and orange as the sun began its ascent, its reflection shimmering across the tranquil waters of the Ganges. A cool breeze carried the faint fragrance of incense, lending the scene an almost otherworldly quality.

Rahul was captivated. The sheer harmony of nature, sound, and spirit overwhelmed him. Reaching for his phone, he began taking pictures, eager to preserve the beauty surrounding him. But even as he captured the sunrise and the serene ghats, he felt a pang of realisation—he hadn't taken a single photograph during his stay in Benaras. Not of the temples they visited, the moments they shared, or even Simran, whose presence had transformed his journey. Turning toward her, he hesitated briefly before asking, *"Simran, would it be alright if I took some pictures of you?"*

She turned to him, a gentle smile playing on her lips. *"Of course,"* she replied, her voice carrying a hint of amusement. But only if we take a selfie together afterward. I need memories, too," she added, her tone playful yet sincere. Rahul agreed, *"Deal. Let's make this morning unforgettable."*

As he raised his phone, Simran stood against the backdrop of the glistening Ganges and the soft, golden light of dawn. She posed naturally, her elegance blending effortlessly with the ethereal ambiance of Subah-e-Banaras. Each frame captured her grace, the beauty of the city, and the unspoken connection between them – a moment suspended in time, forever etched into his heart.

The early morning activity at Assi Ghat wrapped up by 7:30 a.m., leaving behind an air of tranquillity infused with the serenity of the Ganga. Simran turned to Rahul with a thoughtful and exciting suggestion.

"Rahul, how about we quickly drive to Banaras Hindu University?" It's a stunning campus and worth visiting. It'll take 45 minutes to an hour, and then we can head for breakfast."

Photos by the Ganges

Rahul's face brightened instantly. Visiting BHU was on his list, and seeing it now was irresistible. *"I'd love to,"* he replied warmly. *"It would be my pleasure."*

With that, they set off on another memorable journey, ready to explore yet another treasure of Banaras.

A Drive Through Banaras Hindu University

The entrance to Banaras Hindu University (BHU) is a grand gateway to history, culture, and academic brilliance. Its intricate carvings and regal arches are more than just an architectural marvel—they symbolize the institution's century-old legacy. As Simran guided the car through the sprawling campus, Rahul was awestruck by its grandeur and peaceful ambiance.

Lush greenery flanked both sides of the road, offering a calm, almost meditative atmosphere. Here and there, groups of students could be seen cycling to class or walking along tree-lined pathways, their lively chatter adding a vibrant layer to the serene surroundings.

Simran began sharing her thoughts. *"BHU is not just a university; it's a legacy of excellence. Founded in 1916 by Pandit Madan Mohan Malaviya, it was envisioned as a centre that blends modern scientific knowledge with India's cultural and spiritual values."* Rahul listened intently, his gaze shifting between the road ahead and the towering buildings that seemed to echo with stories of the past.

"The campus stretched over 1,300 acres, making it one of Asia's largest residential university campuses. Each corner held its own charm — the Bharat Kala Bhavan Museum with its treasure trove of Indian art, the iconic Shri Vishwanath Temple exuding spiritual energy, and the state-of-the-art library, one of the largest in India."

"Did you know," Simran continued, *"that BHU offers programmes across every imaginable discipline? From arts and commerce to engineering, medicine, and agriculture. The Institute of Medical Sciences and IIT-BHU are particularly renowned."*

As she continued, Rahul noticed groups of students gathered under ancient banyan trees. Their animated discussions reminded her of the intellectual energy that defined the campus. Others walked briskly, books in hand, with clear determination.

"This university," Simran added with pride, *"has produced some of the greatest minds — Dr S. Radhakrishnan, Harivansh Rai Bachchan, and even a former Prime Minister of India, Chandra Shekhar."*

Rahul was captivated by both Simran's narrative and the sights unfolding before him. The cricket ground, the amphitheatre, and the scattered statues of luminaries seemed to breathe life into the university's legacy.

"This is extraordinary," Rahul said, his voice tinged with wonder. *"I never imagined BHU would be this magnificent."*

Simran smiled, happy to see his awe. *"It's not just a place of learning; it's a place of inspiration. It represents the perfect harmony between tradition and modernity."*

Exiting the campus, Rahul remained quiet momentarily, absorbing the experience. His respect for BHU—and Simran's knowledge—had grown immensely. This drive was more than just a detour; it was a journey through the heart of Banaras itself.

Banaras Hindu University (BHU)

LAST BREAKFAST IN BENARAS

Simran smiled as she looked at Rahul. *"Ready for one last breakfast in Benaras?"* she asked, her voice tinged with cheerfulness and nostalgia. Rahul returned her smile, nodding. *"Yes, please, lead the way. I'm ready to savour every last moment."*

Simran had carefully planned their farewell meal at a serene café tucked away from the bustling city streets. Known only to locals, the café was a hidden treasure perched on the banks of the Ganges. Its charm lay not just in its quiet ambiance but also in its spectacular view—a panoramic glimpse of the river glistening under the soft morning sun.

As they entered the café, the blend of freshly brewed chai and baked goods greeted them warmly. The decor was understated yet elegant, with wooden tables, handwoven chairs, and colourful lanterns that reflected the spirit of Benaras. They chose a table by the window, where the tranquil rustle of the Ganges provided the perfect soundtrack to their breakfast.

The morning light played gently across their faces, casting a golden hue on the moment. Simran glanced out at the river, her expression contemplative.

"This place feels timeless, doesn't it?" she said. "It's like the Ganges has a way of holding on to memories."

This is my favourite spot in the city,"

Rahul nodded, his gaze following hers. "It's beautiful, calm and serene," he said. "It's nothing like the chaos we're accustomed to. It's the place that compels you to pause and truly reflect."

They ordered a simple yet hearty breakfast—freshly made parathas, a steaming pot of chai, and a plate of seasonal fruits.

As they ate, their conversation flowed effortlessly, weaving between memories of their shared past and reflections on the present. They laughed over childhood anecdotes, debated over favourite authors, and shared dreams that had long been tucked away. The hours they had spent together in the city seemed to culminate in this moment—a quiet celebration of connection, understanding, and the unspoken promise of staying in touch.

When the plates were empty and the chai cups drained, they ordered the masala chai once again. The reality of parting loomed closer. Rahul looked out at the river, his expression a mix of gratitude and wistfulness. "I don't think I'll ever forget this breakfast," he said, " or *this city.*"

Simran smiled softly. "*Benaras has a way of staying with you,*" she replied. "*And so do the people you share it with.*"

CHAI MOMENTS – SIPPING MEMORIES

Simran sipped on her masala chai, her eyes scanning the horizon, she said. *"Whenever I need clarity or peace, I come here."*

Rahul leaned back in his chair, taking in the serene view. *'I can see why.'*

Simran felt a bittersweet emotion, realising that this might be their last meeting, at least for now. A tinge of regret crept into her thoughts – she had not even invited Rahul to her home. Their last two days had been a whirlwind, attempting to bridge the 40-year gap, yet it seemed they had only scratched the surface of their lives.

Smiling, Simran asked Rahul, *"So, when's your next trip to Benaras?"* Rahul responded with warmth in his voice,*"You tell me,"* he replied.

"Well," she said thoughtfully, *"if you're waiting for my invitation, you know it's always open."*

Rahul nodded. *"I'll plan something soon, but only on one condition – you have to visit Mumbai first. Be my guest."*

Simran paused for a moment, her expression softening. *"I just realised... I haven't even taken you home. You haven't met my family."*

Rahul gave her an understanding smile, his tone reassuring. *"Next time,"* he said gently, *"we'll have all the time in the world."*

Their conversation hung in the air, unspoken promises weaving into the moment's fabric. Neither wanted to say goodbye, yet both knew that this brief meeting had reignited something timeless.

Between the sips, their conversation flowed effortlessly.

"Simran, you've shown me a side of Benaras I never expected," Rahul said. *"But more than that, you've reminded me of a part of myself I'd almost forgotten. These past two days have been... surreal."*

Simran smiled, her eyes reflecting a mix of emotions. *"Rahul, life has a way of bringing us full circle as I had mentioned earlier. We were meant to meet again — not just to relive memories.*

Ties That Bind

A quiet stillness settled over the table as their breakfast neared its end. The soft sounds of the Ganges lapping at the shore seemed to underscore the moment's weight. Simran and Rahul had shared stories, laughter, and memories, but now the inevitability of parting lingered like an unwelcome guest.

Rahul set down his teacup, his fingers brushing the table's edge as if searching for the right words. He looked at Simran, his expression a mixture of determination and vulnerability. *"Simran,"* he began, his voice steady but tinged with emotion, *"I don't want this to be the end. After all these years, we have found each other again, and I don't think I could bear to lose touch again. Can we promise — right here, right now — to stay in touch? To not let life's chaos drift us apart like before?"*

Simran met his gaze, her eyes reflecting a warmth only decades of unspoken connection could hold. Her lips curved into a soft, reassuring smile. *"Rahul, of course."*

Destiny has reconnected after forty years. I don't think anything can separate us now," she said her tone both gentle and resolute . *"Let's promise to check in, to share our lives — even if it's from afar. Because of our bond, it's too precious to let slip away again."* Rahul's face softened, the tension in his shoulders easing. *"You're right,"* he said, nodding. *"It's about intention, distance doesn't matter as long as we make the effort."* For the next few moments, they carefully exchanged contact details — phone numbers, email addresses, and even physical addresses, as though safeguarding every possible avenue to remain connected.

Rahul saved Simran's number with meticulous care, and she wrote her address in a small, tidy script, the ink from her pen deliberate as if sealing their pact.

Simran glanced up, a playful glint in her eyes.

"Now we have no excuses, do we?" she teased, trying to lighten the mood.

Rahul agreeing with Simran

"None at all. And this time, Simran, I'll hold you to it. You'll hear from me so often you might get tired of me."

"Never," she replied softly, her smile unwavering.

As they stepped out of the café, the morning sunlight spilled across the narrow streets of Benaras, painting everything in a golden glow. The city seemed to echo their promise, its ancient walls and flowing river bearing witness to a renewed bond.

Walking side by side, they knew that while the physical distance might separate them, the ties they had strengthened over these few days would remain unbroken, rooted in trust, shared history, and the unyielding resolve to cherish what truly matters.

LEAVING WITH GRACE

The car ride back to Rahul's hotel was quiet; both were lost in their thoughts. As they pulled up in front of the lobby, Rahul turned to Simran.

"Thank you for everything, Simran. For the memories, laughter, and reminding me of the beauty in simple moments."

Simran reached out, her hand resting lightly on his. *"And thank you, Rahul, for the stories, the wonderful songs, and for showing me that some connections never fade, no matter how much time has passed."*

They shook hands, a gesture that now felt far more meaningful than it had two days ago.

As Rahul stepped out of the car and waved goodbye, he felt a strange mix of sadness and gratitude. His time in Benaras was over, but the memories he had made—and the rekindled friendship with Simran—would stay with him forever.

Simran watched him walk into the hotel, her heart full. Life, she thought, had a way of surprising you when you least expected it. And sometimes, it brought you exactly what you needed – a chance to reconnect, heal, and remember the beauty of shared journeys.

With a deep breath, she turned the car around, ready to face her day, carrying the warmth of a rekindled bond with her.

Eternal Elegance – An Inspiring Soul

While leaving Benaras with friends, Rahul sat quietly in his seat inside the car, gazing out of the window at the bustling streets of Benaras below.

With its chaotic charm, the city seemed a perfect reflection of life itself—busy, unpredictable, yet deeply meaningful. His mind, however, was far from the scenes outside. He was lost in thought, marvelling at Simran.

How had she managed it all so effortlessly? He wondered.

From the moment they met at Assi Ghat two days ago, Simran exuded quiet confidence and an unshakeable poise that seemed to guide every moment. She juggled the emotions of a long-lost friendship, the joy of rediscovery, and the depth of their conversations, all while seamlessly showing him the beauty and spirit of Benaras.

Rahul thought about how she had balanced everything so gracefully: the past and the present, the personal and the shared, the light-hearted and the profound.

She had opened her world to him in two and a half days, yet never seemed overwhelmed. She had effortlessly blended her roles: as a host who planned their outings with precision, a friend who listened intently to his stories, and a woman who carried her own share of joys and scars with quiet dignity.

Even when she spoke of her challenges—losing Raj, raising her children alone, and finding her footing again—there was no bitterness or regret. Instead, there was an acceptance, a resilience that shone through every word.

Rahul realised how much strength it must have taken for her to revisit the past, to let him back into her life after so many years. Yet, Simran had done it with such grace that it felt as though no time had passed between them.

Rahul could not help but admire her ability to remain present and live fully in each moment. He remembered their time at Sarnath, where she had shared stories of history and spirituality with the same ease as her own life. It was as though Simran had mastered the art of balance, of embracing the complexities of life without letting them weigh her down.

"She's remarkable," Rahul thought to himself. *"Effortless, yet so intentional in everything she does."*

Rahul leaned back in his chair, a smile playing on his lips. He wasn't sure if he had ever met someone quite like Simran before. Her presence in his life, though brief, had been profound. She had reminded him of the beauty of simplicity, the power of resilience, and the magic of genuine connection. As he prepared to leave Benaras, Rahul made a silent promise to himself: to cherish the memories they had created, to stay connected with Simran, and to carry forward the lessons he had learned from her quiet strength.

For now, though, he simply allowed himself to sit in gratitude, marvelling at the serendipity that had brought them back together after all these years.

Meanwhile, Simran was experiencing a similar wave of thoughts. As she looked out of the window of her car, her mind wandered back to their conversations, the quiet moments they had shared, and the way Rahul's presence had brought a sense of warmth and comfort she hadn't realised she was missing. The reunion had been more than just a nostalgic meeting—it had been an awakening. Simran had felt an old, familiar connection rekindle, but it was more profound than she had expected. There was something about Rahul that felt both comforting and exciting, a mixture of the past and the present, a blend of cherished memories and new possibilities.

As they both departed, their minds were filled with unspoken thoughts. Rahul wondered how Simran felt, if she had been as affected by their time together as he had been. Simran, too, wondered about Rahul's emotions, whether he was feeling the same deep connection she had felt. Neither of them could have predicted how much these two and a half days would change them. As the distance between them grew, both carried with them the memories of Benaras and the possibility of something deeper, something they had yet to fully understand.

THE CONCLUSION – BEYOND THE END

In just two and a half days, their reunion had transformed into something profound—a bond that transcended time, distance, and the limitations of their individual lives. It was a powerful, platonic relationship that neither had anticipated but both came to cherish deeply. The years apart seemed to dissolve in the warmth of their shared moments, as though the universe had conspired to bring them back together when they needed it most.

Rahul found himself reflecting on his feelings with a clarity he hadn't experienced in years. Back in their school days, he had harboured a crush on Simran, a tender affection that he had dismissed as a fleeting infatuation. But now, as he stood in the present, enriched by the wisdom and experiences of life, he understood that what he felt for Simran had always been more than that. It wasn't just admiration for her looks or the quiet charm she carried—it was a deep-rooted respect for who she was and who she had become.

Even so, Rahul's heart remained steadfast. He thought of his wife, whose wisdom had often been a guiding light in his life. She had once told him that *"True love could take many forms and that friendships built on mutual respect and care were among the purest expressions of love."* Her words resonated now, as he recognised the extraordinary gift he had been given: the chance to rekindle a friendship that had been lying dormant for decades.

Rahul smiled inwardly, his heart brimming with gratitude.

He felt as though he had been granted a second chance by destiny, a reward for whatever good karma he might have unknowingly accrued. To find an old, lost friend—someone who had unknowingly held a place in his heart for years—felt like a blessing beyond measure.

In that moment, Rahul realised that what he had with Simran was rare and irreplaceable. It was a friendship built on authenticity, understanding, and a history that neither of them could rewrite but both could celebrate.

And so, as the time in Benaras drew closer to its end, Rahul made a silent promise to himself: to honour this bond, to nurture it, and to ensure that this reunion marked not an ending, but a beautiful continuation of a friendship that had endured the test of time.